*For Gerry Marshall McPake*

# Next to
# ALICE

# Next to ALICE

## Anne Fine

Illustrated by
**Gareth Conway**

Barrington Stoke

First published in 2023 in Great Britain by
Barrington Stoke Ltd
18 Walker Street, Edinburgh, EH3 7LP

www.barringtonstoke.co.uk

Text © 2023 Anne Fine
Illustrations © 2023 Gareth Conway

A CIP catalogue record for this book is available
from the British Library upon request

ISBN: 978-1-80090-174-2

Printed by Hussar Books, Poland

# CONTENTS

# CHAPTER 1

# What's wrong with Alice?

The window next to me had a big crack in it, and everything on my table was blowing about. The caretaker said he'd fix it at lunchtime.

Mr Cates looked round the classroom. The Turner triplets had moved to London. One of them used to sit next to me, and there were the other two empty places.

"Right, Ben," Mr Cates said. "You can sit next to Alice."

1

I didn't want to say out loud that I'd much rather sit next to James. So I went up to Mr Cates' desk and whispered in his ear.

"*What?*" he said. (He couldn't hear me. I was whispering too softly.)

I tried again. "Can I please sit by James? He has a space next to him now as well."

"What's wrong with Alice?" he said. But Matty and Arif, in the front row, were trying hard to hear what I was whispering, so Mr Cates stood up and led me into the quiet corner.

"What's wrong with Alice?" he asked me again.

"Well," I said. "She's a bit ..."

I stopped. I couldn't think how to put it.

Mr Cates frowned at me. "Go on. She's a bit – *what*?"

I still didn't know how to tell him. "You know," I said. "She's a bit ..."

Mr Cates gave me a stern look. "No," he said, "I'm afraid I *don't* know. You'll have to explain. What is wrong with Alice?"

I did try to be tactful. "The thing is," I said, "I just don't think that I'll feel right, sitting next to Alice."

He wouldn't let it go. "Why not?"

I tried to think of a better way of putting it. But in the end I just came out with it. "Because she's *scary*."

I could tell that Mr Cates was really surprised. "Scary? Alice? You think that Alice is *scary*?"

"I don't just *think* she is," I said. "I *know* she is."

"Ben," Mr Cates said. "You're being very silly indeed. Now go and fetch your stuff and sit down right this minute. Next to Alice."

I know when I've lost a battle. I picked up my stuff from my old place and sat down next to Alice.

# CHAPTER 2

# Just sloppy work

I will admit it, Alice acted normal for a while.
She picked up the book I tipped on the floor by
mistake.  She was quite nice about my elbow
sticking out.  She let me use her blue felt-tipped
pen.

Then it began.

It was in Science.  We were meant to be
drawing the shell of a snail.  Mr Cates said we

would have exactly ten minutes to do it. I got mine finished quite fast.

Then Alice started on me. She pointed at my drawing, and she asked me, "Is that *it?*"

I didn't know what she meant. I asked her, "Is *what* it?"

She poked at my sheet of paper with her finger. "This scribble. Is that the best that you can do?"

I tried to defend myself. "I'm not very good at drawing things," I said. "I never have been."

"Nonsense!" said Alice. She flapped the sheet of paper in my face. "This is just sloppy work. Snail shells are smooth and round. This line's so jagged that it looks like a set of steps."

"It's not that bad," I argued.

"It *is* that bad," said Alice. "You'll have to start again."

I told her, "I'm not starting again! There isn't time."

"Then you'll have to sort this out." She set the sheet of paper back in front of me. "First, you can rub out that line and do it again. Properly."

9

I rubbed the jagged line out and drew it again, more rounded.

"That's better," said Alice. Her finger came down again. "And this bit. That is rubbish too. Do it again."

So I rubbed out that line as well, and then the tiny nub of rubber on the end of my pencil fell off onto the floor. I picked it up, but it wouldn't fit back on the end of my pencil. It was all Alice's fault that I'd needed it in the first place, and so I asked her, "Can I please borrow your rubber?"

"I'm busy using it to do my shading," she said. "But I will get you another one."

She leaned forward and poked Teddy in the back till he turned round. "Teddy," she said to him, "can you please cut a chunk off the corner of your fat, giant rubber to give to Ben?"

I thought he'd just say no. If I had one of those fat, giant rubbers, I wouldn't want to cut a bit off it. But Teddy must have been just as scared of Alice as I was because he didn't say anything. He just took his scissors out of his pencil case and carved off a chunk to give to me.

"Thank you," I told him. Then I turned back to Alice and said, "That was really nice of Teddy."

"Nonsense!" said Alice. "You needed some rubber and you didn't have any. He has more rubber than he needs. It was just the right thing for Teddy to do."

I went back to my snail and made a really big effort to do the worst bits of it better this time so Alice wouldn't have another go at me.

When Mr Cates came round, he picked up my sheet of paper and said, "I see your drawing's getting very much better, Ben. This snail is pretty good."

I felt quite chuffed. (But I was still scared of Alice.)

## CHAPTER 3

# That definitely says Bin

It wasn't long before Alice started in on me again. While I was busy writing my four sentences about the snail, she leaned towards me and said, "Why do you make your *e*'s like that?"

I looked down at my paper. I'd written the word *shell*. I'd written the word *pest*. Both of the *e*'s looked fine to me.

I said, "What's wrong with my *e*'s?"

"They're the wrong shape," said Alice. "You make the little hole in them too tall and pointy. They look more like an *i* without the dot." She pointed. "That looks as if it says *shill*, not *shell*."

She pointed to the label on my pencil case. "You've done it here as well, Ben. You've made the *e* in your name look much more like an *i* than an *e*."

## Next to Alice

I looked at the label on my pencil case. It said, **Ben, Room 8** in thick black letters. The *e* looked like an *e* to me.

"You write your letters your way," I snapped, "and I'll write my letters my way. No one has ever said that they can't read my writing."

I turned my head away until I'd finished my four sentences. Then I packed up my stuff and waited for Mr Cates to send us across to Miss Dupont for our next lesson.

We're learning French, and we go across to her room for that because she has the French words for things pinned up all over. The wall. The door. The window. The chair. The whiteboard. (But in French.)

Before we began the lesson, I took out my pencil case and put it on the table in Miss

Dupont's classroom. But we didn't do any writing. We were just saying all the words we knew out loud so that they sounded French. And I forgot to pick up my pencil case at the end of the lesson.

We went back to our own classroom. "Right," Mr Cates said. "Get out your workbooks and carry on from where you ended up yesterday."

I took out my Maths workbook and found the page. I looked for my pencil case, but it wasn't there. I was about to put my hand up when there was a knock on the door.

In came Miss Dupont, and she was carrying my pencil case. She walked across to Mr Cates. "Here," she said. "Someone left this in my room. The label on it says Bin, Room 8. So shall I drop it in?"

With a big smile, she held my pencil case out over the bin, as if she were going to let go of it.

Everyone giggled and some of them looked at me.

Mr Cates grinned at Miss Dupont and put out his hand to take my pencil case. He looked at the label. "Yes," he said, and put a puzzled look on his face. "That definitely says Bin."

"It's mine," I said, and I got up and went to fetch it. When I got back to my place, I said to Alice, "You were right. And now everyone is going to call me Bin, not Ben, for ever."

"No, they won't," Alice said. "Because I won't let them, and they're scared of me."

And she was right. Teddy turned round a minute later. "Hey, Bi—" he started to say.

And then he saw the look in Alice's eye and stopped. "Hey, Ben," he said instead. "Do you still have enough rubber? Do you need any more?"

"See?" Alice said, and winked.

No one else bothered me after that.

(I told you she was scary.)

## CHAPTER 4

# You might as well be eating *hay*

When the bell rang for lunch, Alice stood up and slid her chair in neatly under our table. She turned to me. "Shall we go in together?"

I usually eat lunch with Mohammed and Terry. But I thought maybe Alice had a plan to protect me from anyone who might try to call me Bin. So I said, "That'll be very nice. Thank you."

We walked to the door together. As we went past Mohammed, he gave me a hopeful look. But he didn't say anything. (Maybe he didn't dare.) Terry was in the doorway. As soon as he saw me, he said, "Are you coming to lunch now?"

I opened my mouth to answer, but Alice got in first. "No. Ben is having lunch with me today."

He didn't argue. (Maybe he didn't dare.) "OK," he said, and he and Mohammed went off to the lunch queue together.

Alice and I went after them. Alice chose cheese pasta, and I chose pizza.

We sat down, facing one another, and I started in on my pizza. We get two slices each, with a bit of salad. I pushed the salad aside and picked up the first slice of pizza. They're

shaped like triangles so you can take huge
bites at the pointy end.

Suddenly Alice was rapping her fingers on
the table beside my plate.

I looked up.

"Stop that!" said Alice. "Just stop doing that at once."

I had to swallow everything before I could speak. That took a while. Then, "Stop what?" I asked.

"Gobbling," she told me. "You're just *shovelling* the food in your mouth. You're not looking at it. You're not smelling it. You're probably not even *tasting* it. You might as well be eating *hay*."

I stared at Alice. "*Hay?*"

"Yes," she said. "Like a horse, out of a nosebag."

I took a look at what was left on my plate. And, sure enough, I hadn't really seen the pizza properly.

The topping was all bright and cheery, with cherry red tomatoes, curvy slices of dark green pepper and shiny golden cheese. The crust was a lovely rich brown, with just a few tiny black sprinkles around the edge. The lettuce on the side was a beautiful rich green, with pretty edges, like a flower.

I hadn't smelled the pizza properly either. I bent down to get closer and, yes,

it smelled delicious. Most of it was that I'm-going-to-fill-your-tummy smell you always get with pizza. But there was also a tiny whiff of burnt toast from the crust around the edge.

I had to admit it to Alice. "It does smell wonderful. All warm and cosy."

"Eat it slowly then, so you can taste it," Alice ordered me.

I ate it slowly. Instead of shoving in whole mouthfuls, I took smaller bites. I chewed them well. I paid attention to the little spurts of tomato on the roof of my mouth, the crisp feel of green pepper, and the taste of cheese before I swallowed it.

"Better?" asked Alice.

"Terrific," I told her. "You were right."

"I'm *always* right," said Alice, digging in to her own cheese pasta.

# CHAPTER 5

# It's just a knack

When we came out, the playground was busy.

Some of the rest of the class were playing football. Some were just standing round chatting.

I looked around for Terry and Mohammed, but they were still inside.

There is an alley that runs along the side of our school playground. It's a shortcut for all the houses on Dean Road, and goes to the shops. We have a tall wire fence on our side, but we can see everyone who walks down it.

A woman with a toddler in a pushchair was walking along the alley. She had a huge dog on a long lead, and it was way behind her, stopping to sniff at everything.

Suddenly I heard the loudest whistle *ever*. It came from right behind me.

I turned round, and there was Alice with two fingers in her mouth.

I was amazed. "Was that *you*, Alice?" I asked her.

But she'd run off towards the fence.

The giant dog was rushing to get near to her. He poked as much of his enormous nose as he could through one of the diamond-shaped holes in the fence. And Alice stuck her fingers

through as far as she could, so she could stroke one of his ears.

"Hi, Buster!" she was saying. "Who's a clever dog? Who's beautiful? Who's Alice's best mate?"

He wagged his tail so hard it looked as if it might fall off.

The woman waved. "Hi, Alice!" Then she called the dog. "Come on, Buster. Let's get home."

I waited till they'd turned the corner, then I said to Alice, "How did you learn to whistle like that?"

"Like what?"

I put two fingers in my mouth and blew. All that came out was puffy air. There was no whistle at all. "Like that," I said. "If it had worked. Which it didn't."

"It's just a knack," said Alice. "But I'll try and show you."

We had a sort of lesson out there in the playground.

And then another while we were in the line to go back inside.

And then another in class while we were waiting for Mr Cates to come back from taking Arif to the office when his nose began to bleed.

And then another while we were lining up for P.E.

I kept on practising the whistle in between the races.

Nobody noticed because nobody could hear a thing. I couldn't get the knack at all. I was just rubbish at it.

Then, just as we were going back inside, I did it! Out of the blue. On about my millionth try. A perfect whistle. Really, really loud.

Mr Cates spun around. "Who was that?"

I was so proud of it that I owned up. "That was me. Sorry."

"Well, don't do it again," he scolded me. "Keep that sort of noise for the playground, please. If you're not careful, you might make poor Alice deaf."

# CHAPTER 6

# It's fixed!

We worked hard all afternoon. I was so
grateful to Alice for teaching me to whistle
with two fingers in my mouth that, in return,
I made an effort to write my *e*'s the way she
said. It was much easier than I thought. I soon
got good at it, and I admit they did look better.

When Mr Cates walks round the class, he
often picks up people's work to take a look at it.
After he'd stopped to see Yan's and Tara's, he

picked up mine. He looked at what I'd written, then gave it back to me.

"That's really good," he said. "Your writing's nice and neat and clear. Well done, Ben. Very well done."

I felt dead chuffed. The day was going well And then I looked across to my old place. The caretaker had fixed the window. He must have put in a new glass pane while we were all having lunch in the hall or mucking about outside.

I nearly put my hand up to tell Mr Cates. And then I didn't.

The last half hour went quickly. We had one of the fun quizzes Mr Cates makes up. I knew more than Alice about people in books. And Alice knew more than I did about people in films.

Then the first bell rang. That means we have five minutes to tidy up before the second bell. After that, we can leave. I packed my bag, and blew the bits of rubber off my desk, and sat there, ready.

Mr Cates looked round to see if everyone was tidied up and ready to go. That's when he noticed that the crack in the window next to my old table was gone.

"It's fixed!" he said. "So, Ben, you can go back to your old place tomorrow."

I didn't want to say anything out loud. So I went up to Mr Cates' desk and whispered in his ear.

"*What?*" he said. (He couldn't hear me. I was whispering too softly.) Then, seeing that Matty and Arif, in the front row, were trying hard to hear what I was saying, he stood up and led me into the quiet corner.

This time I said it loud enough for him to hear. "Can I stay where I am, please?"

He looked surprised. "What, next to Alice?"

"Yes," I said. "I think I like it there."

I saw a little smile go over his face. "You don't think Alice is *scary*?"

"Oh, yes," I said. "She definitely is scary. But I want to stay."

"You wouldn't prefer to sit next to James?" Mr Cates said with a big grin. (He thought that he was being really funny.)

"No, thanks," I said. "I really, really want to stay next to Alice."

"Well," Mr Cates said, "you two do seem to work very well together. So if you want to stay there, that is fine by me."

So I went back to my new place and I sat down.

Next to Alice.

Our books are tested
for children and young people by
children and young people.

Thanks to everyone who consulted on
a manuscript for their time and effort in
helping us to make our books better
for our readers.

# More from
# Anne Fine

Anne Fine

How BRAVE Is That?

978-1-78112-243-3

Anne Fine

Gnomes.
Gnomes.
Gnomes

978-1-78112-204-4

Anne Fine

The HAUNTING of Uncle Ron

978-1-78112-285-3

Anne Fine

INTO the BIN
(and out again)

978-1-78112-858-9

# Moving on with
# Anne Fine

# A Remarkable Ear

Illustrated by
Roxana de Rond

Anne

# Anne Fine

# Tales from ...STREET

Anne Fine

# BE NICE
## to Aunt Emma

Illustrated by
Gareth
Conway